Monster Mash Mayhem
in
Acorn Acres

All rights reserved. No part of this book may be reproduced in any form, or by any electronic or mechanical means, including information storage and retrieval systems, without permission in writing from the copyright owner, except for reviewers who may quote brief passages in a review.

First paperback edition: August 2024

ISBN: 979-8-9861997-8-8

Also available as an ebook

Author website: kturnerauthor.com

WELCOME TO
ACORN ACRES

It all started in Acorn Acres, a town that was known for its yearly Halloween bash.

Here, houses were decorated with flickering jack-o-lanterns that were casting spooky shadows.

Children dressed as ghoulish ghosts would run around, darting between cackling witches, as they begged for sweet treats.

The night was abuzz with eerie excitement. Fiona, a fearless fairy, bounced with anticipation as her glittery wings shimmered in the moonlight.

While her friend Gus, a goofy ghoul who was not quite as brave, chomped nervously on a giant lollipop.

Suddenly, a high pitched howl pierced through the air. A mischievous elf, sitting on a tombstone, was laughing with glee.

He had replaced all of the
candy with slimy and jiggly green jellybeans!

The children shrieked! And the sweet treats forgotten, now replaced by the wobbly, jiggly mess.

Little Leo the lion even cried.

But Fiona the fairy came up with a plan. "We need a monster mash," she declared. And with a flick of her wand...

...upbeat music filled the air. Skeletons rattled their bones, mummies came unwrapped, and pumpkins bounced to the beat.

Even the grumpy gargoyle on top of the clock tower couldn't resist dancing along to the music.

Queenie the bat swooped low, her sparkly wings a blur as she danced. Soon, the whole town was swinging and swaying, the jiggly green jellybeans forgotten.

The elf, bored by the lack of frightened faces, watched in confusion. The townspeople, realizing the night wasn't ruined, offered him a plate of spooky treats.

He sheepishly accepted some spiderweb cookies.

United by laughter and music, the townspeople of Acorn Acres danced until the moon climbed high.

Even grumpy Gus the ghoul cracked a smile.

Vampires peeked out from behind trees, mesmerized by the joyous noise.

A friendly werewolf passing by stopped to join the fun, her howl adding a new layer to the music.

The elf, touched by the town's spirit, pulled out his harmonica and joined the band. The music swelled, filling the night with a joyous cacophony.

As the first streaks of dawn painted the sky, the townspeople grew tired. Yawning, they said their goodbyes as they clutched to their leftover treats.

Halloween in Acorn Acres was saved, not by magic, but by the power of friendship, laughter, and a good monster mash. It was a night everyone would remember. A night that proved even the spookiest night could turn into the sweetest treat.

RECIPES

This section is dedicated to creating memorable moments with your kids while also enjoying the Halloween festivities. This selection of recipes are not only easy to make, but guaranteed to bring smiles (and possibly some giggles) to everyone's faces. These treats are perfect for planning your own monster mash, or just bringing a touch of magic to snack time.

Mummy Dogs

Ingredients:

1 package beef or turkey dogs
1 package pizza crust
Mustard or ketchup
Candy eyes *Optional

Directions:

1. Preheat oven to 425° and line pan with parchment paper.

2. Roll out pizza dough and cut into 1/4 inch strips.

3. Stretch the dough around each hot dog, allowing it to crisp cross and overlap. Leave an open space for the eyes.

4. Bake for approximately 20 minutes, then allow them to cool slightly.

5. Use the mustard (or ketchup) to dab on the eyes, or use them to attach the candy eyes.

Monster Fruit Snacks

Ingredients:

Dried Fruit
2 tbsp. Confectioners Sugar
1 tsp. Water, or as needed
Small Candy Eyes

Directions:

1. Arrange fruit on a platter. You can use toothpicks to turn the grapes into caterpillars.

2. Mix water with confectioners sugar to make a thin, sticky icing.

3. Use the icing to attach eyeballs to each piece of fruit. *Optional - Use additional icing to create a mouth.

Banana Ghosts

Ingredients:

Bananas
Popsicle Sticks
White Chocolate
Chocolate Chips

Directions:

1. Peel and cut bananas in half, then insert popsicle sticks.

2. Place bananas on parchment paper and freeze for 1 hour.

3. Dip the bananas in melted white chocolate.

4. Attach the chocolate chip eyes. Then enjoy!

Rice Krispies Treat Monsters

Ingredients:

Rice Krispies
Butter
Marshmallows
Frosting - various colors
Sprinkles
Candy eyes

Directions:

1. Prepare rice krispy treats according to package directions.
2. Allow them to cool slightly, then shape into monsters.
3. Use frosting, sprinkles, and candy eyeballs to create your monster.

No Bake Witch Hat

Ingredients:

Fudge Stripe Cookies
Chocolate Kisses
Honey or Chocolate Icing
Decorating Icing
Sprinkles *Optional

Directions:

1. Place cookie upside down, then use a dab of honey (or icing) to attach the chocolate kiss to the cookie, covering the hole.

2. Using the decorating icing, pipe a bow around the base of the candy kiss.

3. Optional - use the sprinkles to decorate the bow.

Slimy Worms

Ingredients:

Lime flavor gelatin
Gummy worms (or bug of choice)

Directions:

1. Prepare gelatin according to package directions.
2. Pour jello into individual cups or bowls * makes approximately 12
3. Add worms, or other bugs, into the gelatin. You can hang some over the edges so that they stick out of the "slime".
4. Place in refrigerator until gelatin sets.

Witches Brooms

Ingredients:

String Cheese Sticks
Pretzel Sticks
Leaf Spinach *Optional

Directions:

1. Cut the string cheese into 3 pieces.
2. Cut the ends of each piece of cheese to resemble a broom.
3. Insert a pretzel stick into the cheese to represent the broom handle.
4. Optional – Tie a spinach strip around the cheese.

Clementine Pumpkins

Ingredients:

Clementine Oranges
Celery, Cucumber, or Green Apple Slices

Directions:

1. Peel the oranges so that they are still intact.
2. Insert a small slice of celery, cucumber, or green apple to make the stem. This will depend on what you have on hand, as well as your child's flavor preferences.

Jack-o-lantern Fruit Tray

Ingredients:

    Oranges
    Mixed Berries
    Green Apple

Directions:

1. Arrange the orange slices on the platter in the shape of a jack-o-lantern.
2. Insert berries into the mouth and eye slots.
3. Cut apple slices to make the stem. *A piece of celery could also be used f you don't have any green apples.

Zombie Strawberries

Ingredients:

- Strawberries
- Chocolate
- Green Sprinkles
- Candy Eyes

Directions:

1. Wash strawberries and allow to thoroughly dry.
2. Use your preferred method to melt your chocolate (stovetop or microwave).
3. Pull the leaves back, using them as a handle, and dip in the chocolate until coated, then lay on parchment paper.
4. While the chocolate is still wet, dip strawberries in the sprinkles and attach candy eyes.
5. Allow chocolate to set before serving.

Visit kturnerauthor.com to see more books by this author, including these titles and more!

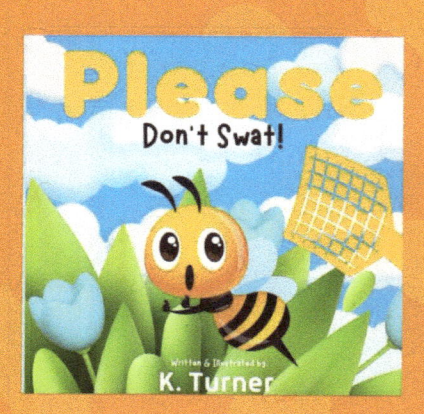

Milton Keynes UK
Ingram Content Group UK Ltd.
UKHW051901230824
447346UK00018B/218

9 798986 199788